triscelle publishing

presents

excerpts from the following
morrigan's brood series books:

morrigan's brood
morrigan's brood book I

crone of war
morrigan's brood book II

madness & reckoning
stories of the morrigan's brood series

Dark Alliance
Morrigan's Brood Book III

Curse of Venus
Morrigan's Brood Book IV

Shards of Light
Morrigan's Brood Book V

By
heather poinsett Dunbar
and
christopher Dunbar

copyright page

Morrigan's Brood Series Chapter Book

Original: February, 2012 / Revised: January, 2016

by Heather Poinsett Dunbar and Christopher Dunbar
Published by Triscelle Publishing
ISBN-10: 1-937341-29-1 - ISBN-13: 978-1-937341-00-8
Edited by Sarah E. Aalderink
Proofread by Jillian Rosenburg and Ruth Davis Hays (certain sections)
Cover art and website by Khanada Taylor
Triscelle Publishing Logo by Dayna Hartley
Arranged by Christopher Dunbar
Excerpts include:

Selected scenes from Journal I
Morrigan's Brood: *Morrigan's Brood Book I*

Selected scenes from Chapter Ten
Crone of War: *Morrigan's Brood Book II*

Selected scenes from Chapter Three
Madness & Reckoning: *Stories of the Morrigan's Brood Series*

Selected scenes from Chapter Six
Dark Alliance: *Morrigan's Brood Book III*

Selected scenes from Chapter Ten
Curse of Venus: *Morrigan's Brood Book IV*

Selected scenes from Chapter Four
Shards of Light: *Morrigan's Brood Book V*

Visit our website and find us on Goodreads, Facebook, Twitter, Shelfari, the Library Thing, LinkedIn, Google+, and WordPress.

www.triscellepublishing.com
www.morrigansbrood.triscellepublishing.com

Heather Poinsett Dunbar
and
Christopher Dunbar
Morrigan's Brood
Morrigan's Brood Book I

Trade Paperback / 312 Pages / List Price $15.99 USD
Also available as an eBook for $1.99

Excerpts include scenes from pages 11 through 18

I am a child of the goddess Morrigan...
I was born in the land of Éire...
and my heart blazes with its fury...
I have lived through the ages...
I seek to right those who have wronged...
I am the maintainer of the Balance...
the Balance must be maintained

Evil reigns throughout much of the Western world in the mid sixth century. Following the collapse of the Roman Empire, a group of blood-drinkers called the Lamia begin the search for a long, lost relic that will restore power to the Roman Empire. After traveling much of the known world, the Lamia discover the relic's location: Ireland. The Lamia invasion forces win a foothold on the island of Éire and hasten their search for this most important relic.

Standing in their way is an outcast Roman general from many ages before, a Briton who would rather tell bawdy jokes than fight, and a young woman who has found her newly acquired lands under siege by a manipulative Lamia seeking vengeance against his oldest foe.

They are not alone.

The Lamia are not the only blood-drinking line on earth. A race called the Deargh Du, who draw their lineage from the goddess Morrigan, will rise up and face the challenges of those who would tip the Balance.

Join the journey, the first in a series of stories revolving around the Deargh Du through the ages.

She gave me gall ink, quills, and several sheets of vellum today. Finally, I have a chance to record my past, what I can remember of it.

However, the legend remains forefront in my mind. So this is my first entry, the Legend of the Deargh Du. It is the story of my line, my people, and the Goddess who created us. The sun rises soon, and the fire is dying, so I must make haste. Here is the tale.

Morrigan, the Tuath Goddess of blood, battle, justice, destruction, and rebirth, gazed upon the expanse of the impending battle below. To the east, She could see the massive army of Milesians disembarking from their crude, yet seaworthy, vessels. The Iberian invaders wanted to try conquering the rich land of Éire again.

As She exchanged glances with the others of Her family, The Tuatha dé Danann, She noticed Her consort, Dagda the All-Father, striding to Her side as they assembled for battle.

Morrigan licked Her lips in anticipation. Soon, spilled blood would mix with the green grass, causing a myriad of delightful scents. Soon, Her ravens could feast again. This time, She would join them.

"Remember what Lady Dana, mother to us all, told us, Morrigan."

"Dearest, how could I forget?" Morrigan felt Her lips turn up into a grimace. Dagda always wanted to be fair, even to His enemies.

"I know that look," Dagda whispered into Morrigan's ear. "You are the Great Balancer. Practice some restraint."

"They are our enemies," She hissed in reply.

"Do not allow your anger at the invaders to overwhelm you. They are our mortal brethren, after all."

Morrigan sighed, before drawing Her blade. While Her consort provided for Her and loved Her, Dagda's little rules about peace and harmony always proved to be highly annoying. Life always involved highs and lows, even for immortals. Tipping the great balance toward good or evil always caused ripples in nature. Such ripples made Her duties more difficult.

Morrigan tilted Her head to the side in order to study the advancing Iberians. "Just another group of invaders." She chuckled to herself. "They will never learn. Perhaps it is time for these rash Milesians to learn not to tread on our lands."

As soon as the Milesians gathered into some semblance of a formation, their leader shouted out a blood-curdling battle cry. At that moment, the enemy charged full force.

Morrigan peered into the leader's dynamic, diamond-blue eyes as he ran, and She could see no fear. Oh, how She would love to see fear in those eyes of his. Perhaps She would have that opportunity soon. "Attack," She shouted as she began to charge.

In answer, the roar of the Tuath chariots echoed through Tara as they galloped over the hills to engage the enemy, but then Dagda shouted, "Hold back," while waving his arms at them, and then the chariots slowed to a walk. Their drivers seemed anxious to charge.

Morrigan ceased Her charge to stare menacingly at Dagda. An itch to plunge Her blade into a mortal heart made Morrigan twitch. She could sense every mortal warrior's heart beat faster and faster as they ran. The scent of blood created by each beating heart became an aphrodisiac for Her bloodlust. Her resolve to stand still and wait for Dagda to make up his mind dwindled in the face of Her hunger to enact vengeance. The Balance had to be maintained.

Finally, Her hunger for rash action won. "I can wait no longer," She cried out. Morrigan then pushed Her way past the other swordsmen and charged the enemy.

She could hear Dagda's grumble of discontent as He and the others joined Her mad dash towards the waiting swords. The roar of the chariots resumed.

Morrigan lost Herself in the tide of redness that overwhelmed the green, sloping hills of Tara. Spears whooshing through the air, swords clanging on other swords and shields, and the screaming, grunting, and shouting of men and women created a sweet song to Her ears.

One had to admire the Mílesians for their fighting skills and bravery. They cut down many immortal warriors. Flush with victory, they continued striking down the Tuaths, unaware of the invincibility of their foe.

However, fear soon flooded the ranks of the remaining Mílesians as they realized that the dead Tuaths returned to life, even after being hacked into pieces. The mortal warriors screeched in horror as the Tuaths impaled them with spears. Soon, sleeting rain hit the Mílesians, pummeling the warriors into submission.

Morrigan's pleasure tripled as the majority of the remaining Mílesians took flight, heading back to their ships on the beach, and began calling on their druid Amairgin for assistance.

In short order, the ships pushed away from the shore, leaving behind the dead and wounded Mílesians as offerings for the carrion birds.

"Come," She called to the others. "We will show them what we do to our enemies."

Dagda held up both hands and replied, "Peace, Triple-One. We shall ask Dana first."

"They are invaders, Dagda," She argued in a hushed tone.

"The Iberian Invaders have no home, remember? The sons of the King Míl left for a new horizon after their enemy took their lands and cattle," Dagda explained, while leaning up against an oak. "Have mercy and let them come forth. Perhaps they will wish for a truce, now. Perhaps they will want to join forces with us against the Fir Bolg. We could use such a worthy mortal adversary to our benefit. Tara and Éire will remain in our hands."

Morrigan sighed. "Fine, work out a truce with our enemies." She then thrust Her sword in the ground and stomped away, watching as the other Tuaths cleared out of Her path. They then formed a circle and began discussing what terms they should offer. She could hear them deciding that they would allow the Iberians either to join them, leave peacefully, or drown in the cold sea.

Fury inflamed Her as She recalled previous invasions. If the others wished to be peaceful, they could. However, She would enjoy tipping the balance against these warriors any way She could. Morrigan cawed as She transformed into a raven and took to the sky, leaving the others behind. Burning hunger grew within.

Morrigan watched cold flecks of snow fall as the Tuaths left the battlefield, leaving the dying Milesian warriors behind on the hillside of Tara. The remaining ice transformed into slush as mud and blood mixed with the sleet. Deep red pools of vitae spilled from the dead and dying Milesian warriors.

Morrigan the raven flew over the carnage. She then paused mid-flight upon seeing a pair of limbs flail about as a warrior tried to pull a spear from his torso. Intrigued, She hovered in closer for a better look. Morrigan soon realized that She beheld the leader of the Milesian force. The spear, with which he struggled, held him to the ground.

As Morrigan watched the warrior's blood escape from his lips, he soon ceased shivering. She could feel great warmth surround his soul as his spirit prepared to depart for the Otherworld. She then cast Her shadow across his broken form and turned the air around them as black as Her feathers. She would not let his soul depart so soon. Morrigan then landed on his chest and stared at the face of the prone figure in the snow. Fear greeted her gaze. Ah, how much She enjoyed finally seeing fear in his diamond-blue eyes.

Morrigan soon hopped to the ground and returned to Her previous form. She then knelt next to his prone figure, leaned forward in order to drown Herself in the aroma of his blood, and then closed Her eyes. She stretched Her neck, letting Her nose guide Her, and began licking away the reddened trails of blood from his skin, losing Herself in the fear exuding from his blood. His terror immersed in Her consciousness, pushing aside the other concerns of battle. She continued to partake of the man's spilled blood.

These new invaders exuded life, and their memories tasted sweet and intoxicating. The coast of Iberia, home of the Milesians, became clear in Her mind. Then, exhilaration swallowed Her whole when another emotion emerged from the warrior. Utter fury.

So delicious.

Morrigan opened Her eyes again, looked up, and noticed that the skies had darkened, signaling the time to return home with the others back to Dagda. She rolled Her eyes, thinking of Dagda's displeasure at Her blood thirst. Defiant, She pulled back a lock of Her hair and turned Her head to regard to the dying enemy once again.

She slid Her tongue across his cold mouth, licking away the remaining blood. As his death drew near, the warrior shook and turned to face Her. She then began to pull out the spear pinning the warrior to the ground, watching him wince as She drew it out inch by inch. Her ears feasted upon his cries of agony. With the spear now withdrawn, She tossed it aside.

"Who..." he whispered, as confusion and anger covered his face.

She snorted a laugh and shook Her head. "I have many names," She whispered. "Some call me Badhbh, Macha, or Neman. For simplicity, most call me Morrigan. You may call me Phantom Queen. I reign over battle, death, destruction, creation, justice, and revenge. I am She Who Maintains the Balance." Morrigan paused and then added, "I watched you during the battle. You were magnificent, Adhamdh," She purred his name.

Surprise greeted Her.

"Yes, I know your name. You were superb, just not good enough to survive my immortal clan."

His ire sweetened his blood as he stared at Her. "I call you by your true name, Witch," he whispered. "Stop taking my essence."

Morrigan's battle apron flapped in the cold winds as She sprawled next to him. She leaned over, traced the remnants of blood surrounding his lips with Her index finger, and raised it to Her mouth. She exhaled as the fury leapt from his blood into Her body. Morrigan then leaned forward and whispered into Adhamdh's ear. "I will do as I please."

Soon, however, his annoying impertinence grew tiresome. "You are nothing but a witch, trying to snatch my soul away to keep me from joining my brethren in the Otherworld."

Morrigan snarled before regained Her senses. "Fine," She hissed. "I will show you that I am no mere witch." Morrigan sat up and tossed aside the bracer on Her right wrist. She then brought Her teeth to Her bare arm and tore away at Her flesh. She crawled over towards Adhamdh and raised Her hand over Adhamdh's face.

"Now, watch a Goddess heal," She whispered as she watched him stare up at Her.

"You bleed as I do," he hissed, "and now I will take your essence back with me to the Otherworld."

Without warning, he latched onto Her mending wrist with his teeth. Adhamdh then drank some of Her blood, before rolling over onto his side, clutching at his stomach, and gagging. His eyes glazed over as he began to giggle and then laugh in a maniacal fashion. His body then began to transform to become more beautiful, more perfect.

Morrigan gasped, horrified that She had failed to prevent this heinous action. She needed to take care of this mistake and send Adhamdh to the Otherworld, but at that moment, She felt his mind tickle Hers. At first, She experienced annoyance at finding Adhamdh within Her mind. However, She soon felt a wordless acceptance and gratitude from him.

Morrigan relished that the former mortal understood Her motives and the reasons behind them. He knew, and yet he did not flee like other mortals or turn away like Her fellow Tuaths.

She never realized that sharing Her essence could be so satisfying. For once, true calm settled over Her. The warrior Goddess closed Her eyes, enjoying the understanding between Herself and the former mortal about the need for balance and the hunger for bloodshed, destruction, and creation.

Adhamdh turned back to Her and began licking away Her bloody wound.

Morrigan watched Adhamdh's wounds close as the harsh reality of what She had done grew more clear. A mortal man had ingested Her immortal blood. Her family, the Tuatha dé Danann, would be furious that She had permitted a mortal to share in Her essence, even though it had been an accident. She could still terminate him, but he seemed to fill a void previously unknown. She could not destroy him now. She needed him. Besides, he could help Her manipulate mankind for Her own satisfaction.

Adhamdh looked at the Goddess with his newly changed, glowing green eyes. Morrigan *turned to watch him, and She felt Her face smooth into a small smile.*

Morrigan clasped Adhamdh's cold hand. "We must go now. There is much for you to learn," She told him as she banished the darkness around them.

They flew far from the battlefield to the hills where the Tuaths held dominion.

The Gods, Goddesses, and fae-folk turned away from Adhamdh. They found him unnatural, but Morrigan enjoyed Her newfound child. Adhamdh's thirst for blood matched Her own, and Adhamdh understood Her bloodlust unlike Dagda or the others.

The Tuaths and faeries called Adhamdh the "Deargh Du". He spent his days hiding from the killing sun, and he hunted with Morrigan at night, feasting on the blood of mortals and the wild creatures of Éire.

As the years passed, others of Adhamdh's kind stalked the night. Morrigan's Brood became legendary, forever caught in the world of mortals with the blood of a Goddess in their veins.

Beautiful, immortal, deadly.

My friend, the young druid, leaves me again to rejoin her teachers. Despite her offers of friendship, there is something in her eyes that chills me to my bones. Still, she offers me the secrets of our race, and I long for the friendship of a companion, even a mortal one. I only fear that my hunger will rise again one night, and she will become my victim.

She promises to teach me more tomorrow night. Perhaps then the thick fog of the past century will clear.

- M.G.P.H

Heather Poinsett Dunbar & Christopher Dunbar

Heather Poinsett Dunbar
and
Christopher Dunbar

Crone of War
Morrigan's Brood Book II

Trade Paperback / 376 Pages / List Price $19.99 USD
Also available as an eBook for $1.99

Excerpt includes scenes from pages 203 through 210

I am a child of the goddess Morrigan...
I was born in the land of Éire...
and my heart blazes with its fury...
I have lived through the ages...
I seek to right those who have wronged...
I am the maintainer of the Balance...
the Balance must be maintained

The Lamia expeditionary force has gained a foothold in Éire and has formed an alliance with a powerful Irish chieftain and his malevolent mother. To reinforce them, a massive Lamia army, which is departing Rome, will soon give them enough power to conquer Éire and find their lost treasure.

Will the Deargh Du and their newfound friends be able to protect Éire from the invaders, or will the Deargh Du's suspicion of other blood-drinkers allow their enemies to be victorious?

Continue the journey... the second in a series of stories revolving around the Deargh Du through the ages.

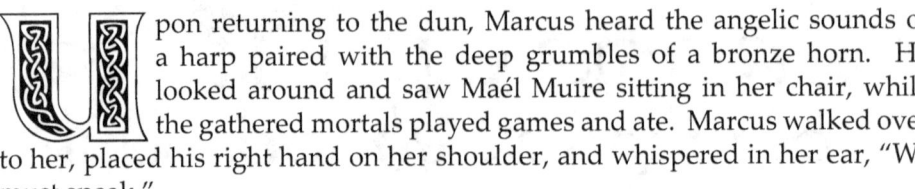

chapter ten

Béal Átha an Fheadha

Upon returning to the dun, Marcus heard the angelic sounds of a harp paired with the deep grumbles of a bronze horn. He looked around and saw Maél Muire sitting in her chair, while the gathered mortals played games and ate. Marcus walked over to her, placed his right hand on her shoulder, and whispered in her ear, "We must speak."

Maél Muire did not immediately look up at Marcus, as she seemed entranced with the performance. "Berti should be a bard," Maél Muire informed him in a far-away voice. "He is full of good stories." She then turned her head to regard Marcus and seemed to notice the frown he wore. "What is it?" she asked in a more focused tone.

He leaned closer to her and whispered in her ear, "Your friend, Mac Turrlough, conspires with the Lamia, Maél Muire. I followed him to his mother's home where he spoke of them. He even mentioned Mandubratius."

Marcus heard Maél Muire inhale audibly, prompting him to pull away. As he drew back, he noticed her moss-green eyes grow wide. "I tried to follow him," he explained, "but his mother found me. She is... strange."

"I know. She was normal as any druid, once," Maél Muire replied. "She taught my aunt a great deal. However, her husband was the victim of a Deargh Du in transformation, and Seosaimhín never recovered."

"Yes, the first night," Marcus murmured, remembering his own experience. "I could not find Mac Turrlough after we spoke. I had hoped I could follow him to Mandubratius. However, Mac Turrlough disappeared into the mists. Strange... He seems to care for you, though. I would continue your relationship with him for now. Make no promises, but do not turn him away." Marcus contemplated how to explain the next bit of intelligence, but sometimes it was best to just spit it out. "Also, Seosaimhín believes you to be pregnant. Are you?"

Her skin turned pale, almost bloodless. "Could you get me a drink?"

"Of course," he answered, before getting up for some mead.

"I hope these warriors will understand the concept of 'fas est et ab hoste doceri'," Marcus heard Claudius murmur as they neared the mist-covered fields, which grew obscured with mist.

Mac Alpin grumbled. "More Latin-talk. You two do remember that I do not know Latin very well."

"'It is right to learn, even from the enemy'," Marcus translated, feeling the quote from Publius Ovidius Naso fit his training situation. Of course the question remained... could the warriors of Éire learn from a former enemy?

"I fear that sentiment will be hard for these warriors to accept," Arwin suggested. "On the other hand, it will be amusing to watch this."

Soon the mist parted, revealing Maél Muire holding an oak branch.

"Chieftain Maél Muire," Marcus greeted her.

"This is not as easy as it looks," she explained after closing the distance with the blood-drinkers. "Then again, your job seems much more complicated." Maél Muire seemed to accentuate her comment by nodding toward the gathering of Deargh Du that milled about in the field.

"Two hundred and fifty Deargh Du, plus we Britannic and Alban blood-drinkers," Claudius observed aloud as he rubbed his chin. "Mandubratius has nearly twice that."

"'In war, numbers alone confer no advantage'," Marcus added, hoping he exuded confidence. "Some eastern philosopher-warrior said that." After a few moments, he could see a figure he recognized in the distance. "It's Sáerlaith." Although she did not stand alone.

He then started walking towards the her and the other Deargh Du. He heard Maél Muire wish them luck as Marcus, Claudius, and Mac Alpin, with the other Britons in tow, made for the waiting Deargh Du warriors. These looked different from the Deargh Du of Ard Mhacha, appearing less like druids and more like the battle-hardened warriors he remembered seeing as a mortal first landing on Éire.

"Perhaps you should do that dark clouded mist thing, you do," Claudius suggested.

"Aye, we can listen to them then," Mac Alpin stated.

As Marcus closed his eyes and called down the darkness, Claudius and Mac Alpin walked behind Marcus, and each blood-drinker placed a hand on one of Marcus' shoulders. The three seasoned warriors then crept in closer to the gathered forces. As they approached, Marcus could hear the banter amongst Sáerlaith and the other Deargh Du.

"Sáerlaith, where are these great warriors you promised?" one yelled.

"They will be here soon, Idwal," Sáerlaith replied. "I suggest you all sober up and think over what you must do to take care of the Lamia."

"I know what should be done," the one known as Idwal hissed. "Bring in someone who is truly interested in solving the problem. I can handle the training. I fought with Cu Chulainn and The Red Branch."

The gathered Deargh Du issued forth a derisive hiss.

"Idwal, you wish you were with the Red Branch!" a woman shouted in reply. "That was a bit before your time. Sáerlaith, where is this Roman Deargh Du we hear murmured about on Manannán Mac Lir's breeze? Where are these blood-drinkers from Britannia and Alba?"

"They will arrive soon," Marcus heard Sáerlaith reply. As he watched through the edge of the blackness surrounding him and his friends, he could see her staring at the gathering. "I know you all are suspicious," she continued. "Just remember, Morrigan whispers Her wishes to the council." However, her words appeared to be wasted.

"You doubt my skills, Ula?" Idwal shouted before giving Ula a push.

Ula laughed before whirling about and twisting Idwal's arm around his back. "I doubt nothing about your lack of skills." The two Deargh Du separated and then began circling one another, growling.

Marcus heard Sáerlaith sigh as she backed away from the center of the clearing, while the others surrounded the challengers, waiting for the bragging to stop and the true fight to begin. Soon, a blinding display of fist fighting ignited between the combatants.

Now is the time.

Marcus extended the darkness to surround the other Deargh Du. He, along with Claudius and Mac Alpin in tow, then flew over the blinded Deargh Du and hit Idwal in the face, sending him sprawling backwards to the ground. Marcus cleared the black mist, revealing himself and his two companions. He could see the other Deargh Du stand in shock, while Sáerlaith smiled and shook her head.

"I am Marcus Galerius Primus Helvetticus," Marcus yelled while crossing his arms over his chest and staring at the sputtering crowd of Deargh Du. "These are my associates, Claudius Metrius Sertorius of the Sugnwr Gwaed and Arwin Mac Alpin of the Ekimmu Cruitne."

The gathering erupted in general grumbles and few mutters of 'cursed ones', which he chose to ignore for the moment.

"Sáerlaith requested that I teach you all that you need to know in order to defeat the Lamia. I have some experience in the realm of Roman tactics. I arrived in Éire during the first invasion of Britannia, leading the seventh legion under Julius Caesar. I recently have been spying on the Lamia, pretending to be one of their own."

A Deargh Du near him scoffed, "If you were on your way to Britannia, how did you end up in Éire?"

Marcus strode over to the proud warrior who asked the question and stared down at him. "Our general had requested that I take the mortal whelp known as Mandubratius to his friends on the western coast of Britannia. That whelp now holds the leadership of the Lamia."

"You wish our trust to belong to someone such as this bastard of Morrigan?" another Deargh Du queried while staring at Sáerlaith. "Our battle methods are not questionable. They work." To Marcus, the Deargh Du added, "I will not fight in an army with this mistake."

"Alright then," Marcus replied. He could not help but smirk at the gathered warriors. "If you wish, you can go back to your homes and villages... that is if one of you can defeat me in single, unarmed combat." He observed several Deargh Du staring at him with murder in their eyes. Wishing to provoke them further,

Marcus took a few steps closer to some of the more battle-hardened warriors... to one in particular who seemed ready to accept Marcus' challenge.

"Then toss aside your sword and this armor of yours," the warrior replied. While the warrior spoke, his eyes burned bright green.

Marcus smiled at the warrior and then turned back to regard his friends. He began removing his weapons and handed them to Mac Alpin. He then walked to the edge of the circle, removed his armor, and placed it on the ground. He then turned around and met the Deargh Du's stare.

The Deargh Du warrior yelled a battle cry and raced towards him.

Marcus stepped aside at the last moment, grabbed the blood-drinker's right arm, and elbowed him in the throat. He heard a soft inhalation from the impact. He then pulled up the Deargh Du, getting a good look at the pale, pretty features, and punched him with his right fist. Marcus watched the unconscious warrior land ten feet away. The stranger left behind five teeth, including a fang.

Three other Deargh Du warriors raced toward Marcus, snarling, and so he fell flat on his back with the sudden impact. He then kicked at the middle one, who collapsed into a ball, moaning. Next, Marcus shot out his arms in a rapid motion, and then the other two tripped and staggered back towards him as he leapt back to his feet.

Marcus stepped in front of the smaller one and pulled him off balance by kneeing him in the on the inner-side of the warrior's left knee and yanking down on his left shoulder, dislocating it. He then felt a fist from the other warrior connect with his chin.

Marcus looked up into the eyes of two others warriors, who joined the one remaining warrior, wielding knives that reflected the moonlight. He soon felt a strange pull within, and then without the concentration he usually needed, the darkness cascaded down around him and the warriors who surrounded him. He then flew up and over one of the knife-wielding combatants and managed to plunge the warrior's knife into her own stomach.

Marcus lost himself in the momentum of the battle as other Deargh Du warriors joined in the fray, enraged that a Roman had defeated their friends with trickery, Marcus reasoned. He attacked from the air, from chest-level, and from the ground, never from the same place. He struck with fists, elbows, arms, and the warrior's own weapons, careful not to kill his opponents.

When he could sense no other challengers stood to face him, he sent the darkness away. The moonlight skies returned, revealing a dozen moaning warriors on the ground who clutched at their wounds. He then noticed Sáerlaith smirk. Marcus dusted off his hands and looked back into the sea of beautiful faces, those who had not challenged him. "So, does anyone else want to go home now?" he queried.

The Deargh Du stared back at him as if uncomfortable. No one came to the aid of the fallen warriors to offer them blood or healing.

"So, now you wish to stay," Marcus continued. "When I first started in the

Roman legions, I was taught that a disorderly mob is no more an army than a heap of building materials is a house." Marcus walked away from the pile of moaning bodies towards his armor, which he donned.

Mac Alpin, Claudius, and the other Ekimmu Cruitne and Sugnwr Gwaed, who had waited at the fringe of the crowd of Deargh Du, pushed through the Deargh Du to gather in front of him.

Marcus collected his weapons from Mac Alpin and then turned to regard the Deargh Du. "You do not need to like me. I am not here to be a friend to anyone. However, I am here to mold you into an effective fighting machine that can go against an army bred for conquest. I need ten volunteers. Those who wish to volunteer can walk to the front."

He looked around the field, hoping to see a hand raised, but instead the only movement he witnessed was Sive holding what appeared to be a branch of rowan. No Deargh Du moved forward. "So no one wishes to volunteer?" Marcus queried, feeling a hint of a smile curl his lips. "Well, what method of persuasion should I use to elicit ten volunteers? I suppose I could offer a dozen heads of cattle to each of you who walks forward."

Beautiful eyes stared away from his, studying the ground, the trees, the Ekimmu Cruitne, the Sugnwr Gwaed... anything to avoid meeting his gaze.

"Well?" Marcus chuckled. "Then perhaps twenty pieces of silver? Mead?"

The still and silent Deargh Du yielded no answers.

"I see a pattern," Marcus said, before pacing amongst the gathered Deargh Du. "Well then, if such material matters do not motivate you, I will select volunteers." He then started to his right, following the path of the sun. Any Deargh Du who managed to meet his stare, he selected, until he reached the eighth.

A low, feminine voice drawled, "I wish to volunteer."

He turned to stared into the fierce, blue eyes of a plaited, blonde warrioress. Marcus raised a brow. "You have an open invitation. What is keeping you?" He watched her motion to another, and together they raced to the smaller gathering. Marcus followed them. When he reached his friends, he announced, "Mac Alpin, you will handle the training of these ten, who are now in positions of leadership."

The Ekimmu Cruitne rubbed his hands in delight as they prepared to depart. "Do not worry, for your fates are already sealed," Mac Alpin stated. "You ten are bound to me now. I will make it as painful as possible." He then turned on his heel and yelled at the ten lucky Deargh Du to follow him.

Marcus faced the other Deargh Du and stated, "The rest of you will start by getting your bodies and minds prepared to fight." He then called for Claudius over his shoulder.

His former lieutenant in the tenth legion ran over to him and said, "Yes gener... Marcus." Claudius aborted a Roman a salute and lowered his right arm.

Marcus closed the distance with Claudius, and then in a hushed voice he said, "Besides your usual duty in my personal guard, I have another task, one that I know is beneath you, but I need to ask it of you regardless. We are in need of someone to assist me in getting these warriors to learn how to stand in straight lines."

"The honor is to serve," Claudius replied.

Marcus felt the cool, early morning breeze blow through the night sky, as the horizon began to brighten to the east. The calls of birds echoed through the whispering trees as he, the rest of the warriors, and the others who accompanied them walked back towards the dun.

A few minutes before, Marcus had dismissed the Deargh Du soldiers, instructing them to dig holes in the ground to serve as their shelter from the sun. Now, their grumbled complaints rivaled the sounds of the waking day.

He followed Claudius, Mac Alpin, and the druids on the path leading towards the dun. Marcus then noticed Maél Muire stray from the group, walking at a slower pace, with her head down as if lost in thought. Just as the others disappeared into the shadows that still remained, Marcus edged back towards her, matched her pace, and gazed into her now upturned eyes. It seemed they reflected a growing astonishment. Perhaps the large gathering of Deargh Du and druids had been too much for her to take.

He broke eye contact with Maél Muire and then stared ahead of them, thinking about how to prepare for the next evening's work, when she interrupted his thoughts.

"I have never seen this side of you," she said in a soft whisper. "Marcus, how could you be so brutal? Your actions were vicious, even for a Gael, and I have seen many bloodthirsty Gaels."

"As a general under the command of Julius Caesar, I had not the patience or tolerance for insubordination, or the outright defiance that these Deargh Du display, and–"

"You were a general?" He could barely hear her queried interruption.

He stopped walking and turned to face her. "I have never lost a battle using these tactics, Maél Muire. My men were part of a unit, and we fought for the cause of Rome. We were all unified in our struggle." He paused for a moment. "I am just doing what I feel needs to be done to save Éire. I do not wish to offend you, but the methods I use yield winning results." Marcus chuckled softly. "Besides, their limbs will grow back."

As he started walking again, she paced in step with him, her shorter legs having to take two steps to make one of his.

"How are Berti, Sitara, and Edward?" he asked.

"They are all doing well," Maél Muire answered, though her tone seemed dismissive, as if she desired to speak on a more pressing topic. "We are going to see my aunt and uncle tomorrow so they can check on Sitara's progress. My knowledge in such things is limited."

A pregnant pause grew between them, but soon she asked, "So, how did you become Deargh Du? Why did Morrigan choose a Roman general? Before you, She only blessed the people of Éire with Her gifts."

Marcus sighed while trying to think of an appropriate half-truth. "Maél Muire, I do not know why the Goddess allowed it," he began to explain. "They left me to my own devices, abandoning me to the mortal world."

"So, did the Deargh Du encounter you within Rome, or were you in Éire? When did your transformation take place?"

"I was in Éire," he answered, hoping she would end the interrogation soon.

"When?" she asked. "Where in Éire?" Maél Muire's questions grew more demanding.

"Near Loch Garman," Marcus answered, "nearly six hundred years ago."

He heard Maél Muire drag her feet in a sudden stop. He then turned around to regard her and saw pain etched across her face.

She drew her sword from its sheath and stared at him while moving into a defensive posture. "You were the Roman general who led the invasion there? You ordered the slaughter of the villagers and the druids in that grove?" Tears welled up in her green eyes.

Marcus said nothing, and yet he knew his posture exuded the guilt he felt.

"And you participated? To this day, there are still stories told of your cruelty." He heard her voice grow wrought with emotion. "They spoke of a Roman general in red and gold whose dual swords raged like lightning strikes, a man possessed by the elements and driven with bloodlust."

Marcus opened his mouth to speak, but she continued. "They invented words in our ancient tongue to describe you." She finally grew silent, awaiting his answer. Her eyes now swam with angry and fearful tears as her palpable emotions intensified.

"Yes, that was me," he confirmed, "when I was mortal. I had my reasons for being that way, Maél Muire."

She uttered a soft cry. "I will not hear another word from you. I–"

"Please hear my story before you judge me," Marcus pleaded. "Caesar made a deal with Mandubratius. We pledged our assistance in helping him regain his lands in Britannia. We invaded Britannia, yet there was a stalemate, and Mandubratius led one of our ships to what we all believed to be the western coast of Britannia. Instead, we found ourselves in Éire, and while ten of us went scouting for Mandubratius' comrades, the local chieftains and their warriors killed my men. The soldiers were scattered over the beach, their bodies desecrated."

Marcus stopped speaking to let her brain digest the information. He then continued, "The Britons were nowhere to be found. The one survivor of my men told me, before he died from his wounds, that Mandubratius' friends had spurned us and joined with the Gaels. We then turned our fury on Mandubratius." He decided to leave out the details of the punishment. "Then, we went to find the killers, burning the forest as we marched, killing whatever dared cross our paths. It was about justice, Maél Muire, justice for my dead men. Don't you desire justice?"

"But you still have not told me how you became Deargh Du!" Maél Muire raged. "The bards say Morrigan Herself came down to slay the invaders! Why did She choose you? How could a murderer such as you be accepted by Her? I cannot believe this!" Maél Muire then pointed her sword at him. "If you did not have the blessing of the Council, I would insist you leave immediately. However, because you do, I will only insist that you not present yourself in my dun. Bearach will bring your things to your dark hole," she hissed.

Marcus watched Maél Muire storm off, her jaw and fists clenched in utter fury.

(Continued on page 210)

heather poinsett dunbar
and
christopher dunbar

Madness & Reckoning
stories of the morrigan's brood series

Trade Paperback / 72 Pages / List Price $4.99 USD
Also available as an eBook for $0.99

Excerpt includes scenes from pages 24 through 26

i am a child of the goddess morrigan...
i was born in the land of éire...
and my heart blazes with its fury...
i have lived through the ages...
i seek to right those who have wronged...
i am the maintainer of the balance...
the balance must be maintained

madness

Following the events of 564 CE, madness strikes one of the Lamia's most important personages. Can the Lamia march on, or will this insanity cast them into civil war?

reckoning

Following the events of 564 CE, the Deargh Du must come to grips with change or see old strife resurface, which could tear the Deargh Du apart.

Heather Poinsett Dunbar & Christopher Dunbar

chapter three

andubratius exhaled, reveling in his relaxation. He thought once no baths could compare with those in Rome. However, Byzantium, with its warmer climate, proved better than he believed it could be.

Julian would win this battle against the Persians, and this victory would elevate the Emperor's power and influence.

Mandubratius closed his eyes and soaked up the warm currents of the bath. If he desired it, the slaves would bring wine, whores, and even blood.

The last few years had been most pleasurable. Mandubratius had shaped and formed Julian like clay between his fingers. Part of Mandubratius wished he had travelled to Persia with the Emperor's army. If only Felician could witness this triumph, yet his foolish sponsor remained in Rome.

Mandubratius decided that perhaps he would call for a prostitute... the warm water and the promise of victory proved to be quite an aphrodisiac. However, before he could call for a slave to bring him a few women to satisfy his sexual urges, a voice as cold as ice water pierced his contentment like a dagger.

"Are you quite enjoying yourself, Mandubratius, or are you using that loathsome name your barbaric parents gave you when your mother squeezed you out of her often plowed loins?"

Mandubratius shivered, but he hoped Felician had not witnessed his surprise. With as much nonchalance as he could muster, Mandubratius opened his eyes and watched the other Lamia slide into the bath opposite of him.

"Oh, this is quite wonderful," his sponsor purred.

"This is indeed a surprise. I didn't expect you here, Sponsor." Mandubratius did his best to bury his alarm, as Felician would exploit any hint of weakness.

Felician stretched in the water. "I didn't think that you liked hot water, as I seem to remember your preference for ice-covered streams."

Mandubratius waited, since Felician still had not made eye contact with him. His sponsor then leaned back against the wall of the bath.

Mandubratius concentrated his senses on the others within the building to see whether other Lamia had accompanied his sponsor, yet Mandubratius perceived nothing but mortals... for now, at least.

"For some reason, I doubt you were expecting me. I think this is your attempt to hide your surprise. If you were expecting me, you would not be alone and naked in a bath house, would you?" Felician asked.

Mandubratius attempted to compose himself without revealing his unsteadiness. "You make it sound as if I should fear you."

"Fear me?" Felician asked, false incredulity in his tone.

Mandubratius wondered whether he should risk asking his sponsor what was on his mind.

Why is he here?

Mandubratius continued to ask himself that question deep within the recesses of his mind, though fearful that Felician could eavesdrop on his more protected thoughts.

"Have I done anything that would compel you to travel to Byzantium?" Mandubratius cringed inside, afraid that his sponsor would strike him, but instead, Felician smiled.

"Awvarwy, Awvarwy, Awvarwy... Gods below, I hate that name. It's so ... clumsy and foreign. Awvarwy, when I first found you, I did not plan to sponsor you... I merely wanted to drain you dry, despite the fact that there was so little vitae left in you. Even if I had been seeking out new Lamia to sponsor, I simply would not have felt that any Briton could have risen to prominence in the Lamia, but Amata wanted a toy, and I owed her..."

He wondered how Felician could be indebted to Amata.

"... so I sponsored you and trained you. I spent centuries grooming you as my protégé, and then you rewarded my charity with betrayal."

Mandubratius noticed his sponsor's cold blue eyes begin to turn red. He felt like arguing with Felician, but Mandubratius knew it would be best to remain silent. Felician had beaten that fact into him many times over the years.

Felician did not blink, and so Mandubratius' dread grew as he considered the possible reasons why his sponsor had come here.

"There was a time when you did not know when to hold your tongue, and I would have struck you for such behavior. So, Mandubratius, I shall give you leave to speak. I am certain you would like to explain yourself."

Mandubratius steadied himself again. "For what reasons do I need to explain myself?" he queried while attempting to appear calm.

Felician smashed his fist against the water, splashing them both. "You betrayed me!" his sponsor growled. Felician's eyes turned completely red, but after a moment of intense agitation, the elder Lamia regained his composure. Mandubratius felt a strange satisfaction knowing he had cracked his sponsor's calm facade.

"You sided against me. You helped that mortal... Julian... rise to power when you knew that I wanted a theocratic empire under the rule of the Pope, who I control. Everything was perfect! Our wealth, power, and influence grew by leaps and bounds! Since I brought that damnable Jewish cult to Rome, the masses have remained under our domination!"

Mandubratius tried not to roll his eyes. That cult had arrived in Rome on its own, but he had to admit that Felician had a strong influence in its dogma and its corruption.

"But you had to get that... puppy to bound into power, and you convinced it to become an apostate, of all things, and reject the faith! What were you thinking,

Awvarwy?"

Mandubratius remained silent and adjusted his gaze to stare at the water, instead of meeting Felician's stare. Mandubratius then heard Felician grumble under his breath.

"Permission to speak," Mandubratius requested in a clipped, precise tone.

In response, Felician waved his hand in an impatient manner.

"Was I not doing what you taught me to do, to stand on my feet and gain power and influence, Sponsor? Is this not the way of the Lamia?" he asked Felician.

His sponsor leaned forward. "The way of the Lamia is to follow your Consul, who is me. You went against me, Awvarwy!"

After a moment of rage, Felician returned to his calm demeanor and closed his eyes. "Well, Mandubratius, despite your digressions against me… I forgive you." Felician then reopened his eyes, stared at Mandubratius, and smiled.

Mandubratius sucked in his breath as the realization dawned on him that Emperor Julian was dead.

"Yes, Julian is dead," Felician stated as he continued to smile. "He was killed by one of his own soldiers who believed this to be a death ordained by God, although some will believe the Persians killed him."

Mandubratius wondered for a moment whether Felician planned to kill him next.

"Awvarwy, I have spent so much time training you, so I will not toss you aside for such a small inconvenience. It is just one, miniscule Emperor, after all. You show much promise, but I fear that you have demonstrated that you will never amount to anything. You will never accomplish more than I have. You are a failure, but I must accept some blame for that. However, your ineptitude as a Lamia could be because you are a Briton."

Felician scooted over to Mandubratius and then leaned his face closer so he stared into Mandubratius' eyes. "My only regret is that I should have killed you that fateful night on the beach in Éire. Your bath is over, and it is time for you to return to Rome. There is nothing left for you here, now."

Felician climbed out of the bath and, with his back turned to Mandubratius, began to pat himself dry.

Mandubratius felt relief that Felician was unable to see the tear in his eye.

(Continued on page 26)

Heather Poinsett Dunbar
and
Christopher Dunbar
Dark Alliance
Morrigan's Brood Book iii

Trade Paperback / # Pages 360 / List Price $16.99 USD
Also available as an eBook for $3.99 USD

Excerpt includes scenes from pages 98 through 103

I am a child of the goddess Morrigan...
I was born in the land of Éire...
and my heart blazes with its fury...
I have lived through the ages...
I seek to right those who have wronged...
I am the maintainer of the Balance...
the Balance must be maintained

Following their war against the Deargh Du, the Lamia have refocused their efforts toward controlling the Church of Rome, using it as a tool for amassing greater power and wealth. In Éire, fissures have formed in Deargh Du society, threatening to break apart the once firm foundation of the Balance.

In the midst of these events, a new menace threatens the Balance within the Holy Roman Empire as vicious murders of both mortals and blood-drinkers spread throughout the empire like wildfire. Can a hastily formed alliance between archenemies thwart this new menace, or will festering hatred bring about the empire's doom?

Continue the journey... the third in a series of stories revolving around the Deargh Du through the ages.

chapter six

Francia, 801 C.E.

(Starting from Page 98)

Marcus started counting the guards again. Their numbers had increased. The scents of his associates mingled in with the mortals. He sensed the guards toss Claudius into the cell next to his.

"Claudius," Marcus whispered. "Claudius!"

"Marcus?" Claudius said, raising his voice so they could hear each other through the wall. "Is that you?"

"Shhhh… what happened?"

"We tried to get to the dungeon through the garrison, but we were caught, because we failed to follow protocol," Claudius answered. "We thought about taking time to study the guards' habits, but Mac Alpin thought that might be difficult if you could not fly out. Do you have the strength to escape with us?"

"Not without seriously injuring someone," Marcus murmured. "Frankly, I do not think that would be the wisest plan to follow. I have not fed in two nights. There are nearly forty guards here. I do not want to kill the emperor's men needlessly, though without feeding soon, I'll have little control. Besides, we may need them to assist with the Strigoi. What is the backup plan?"

Claudius chuckled. "This is the backup plan, Marcus. Oh, wait. Amata says she has contacts here. What should we do in the meantime?"

"Conserve your strength. It does not look like it will be easy feeding with so many eyes watching us."

"Very well," Claudius conceded.

Mandubratius wandered into the palace, just beating the daylight. He waved away his entourage, which fast approached him. "Tonight. Just let me have some rest until tonight," he said, hoping that manipulation and mind-bending would not be necessary.

He followed the secretary to his guest quarters and collapsed on the bed, grateful again for a windowless room.

Mandubratius awoke the next evening to the delirious and delicious sensation that women waited for him. It would probably be nothing more than a dream, but he did have his hopes. He inhaled and closed his eyes. One of the visitors could be Amata. The thin threads of recognition tugged at his memory and confirmed his suspicion. The other person must be a stranger.

Mandubratius walked into the sitting room in his linen, long-sleeved tunic that went to his knees. He smiled at Amata and then turned his gaze to the other woman. Dark red, flame-colored curls and green eyes met his stare and did not blink.

He smiled at Maél Muire and almost laughed as she gave up in their staring battle and turned away from his eyes as if she became shy. He tried to make his body behave. He had half a mind to send Amata outside and then pick up his long, lost treasure in order to spend the evening punishing her for her cruelty at their last meeting. The tiny pinch of anger that remained melted away at seeing her in a dress the color of a woman's tender blushes. He trained his eyes on the wall behind her.

"So," he began, feeling a smile purse his lips. "What brings you two dazzling goddesses into my midst?"

Amata opened her mouth and then glanced at Maél Muire.

"I wish I were here to rip out your heart and feel the blood trickling through my fingers," Maél Muire revealed with a slight grimace, "however, there is an alliance now between my kind and yours, and we need your assistance. When we first arrived in your quarters, I almost left, but Amata told me you would help us in our time of need. Let it be known that I am only here, speaking with you, to rescue my oldest friends. To give this long tale some brevity, I suppose I am here to kiss your arse," Maél Muire finished. He noticed her grimace fade into a resolved smirk.

"How fortunate for me that you and yours allied with us," Mandubratius purred. He sat down in a chair across from theirs.

"So, the both of you need help from me." He could but continue to smile. "How was your journey, Amata?"

"Ma—"

"Michael," he interrupted her, holding up a finger.

He noticed Maél Muire stare at Amata as if confused.

"Excuse me," Amata said with a smirk. "Michael, this is Máire."

"Máire, what an odd name," he said. "Bitterness really does not suit you," he said to Maél... Máire.

"Neither does your new name suit you," she snapped, and then her mouth moved back into an uneasy smile.

"Are you not going to inquire as to what assistance we need, my Lord Emissary?" Amata asked.

"Of course," he answered, pretending to be distracted. "How may this humble servant of God assist you?"

He almost started laughing at the confused look upon Máire's face.

"It would seem that the inspector general of the Gendarmes has caught your old friend Marcus. They arrested him two nights ago." Amata folded her hands over her dress.

"Marcus! Captured by a mere mortal gendarme?" He started to laugh.

"Last night, while trying to rescue Marcus, Patroclus and three of our companions were also caught and imprisoned," Amata added.

Mandubratius continued laughing and shook his head, trying to control his outburst. "This is a wonderful tragic comedy of errors that even Plautus himself could not have conjured. Why doesn't Marcus simply knock down the door and release himself?"

He watched Maél... Máire open her mouth to answer.

"I know," he smirked. "Marcus wouldn't dare endanger a mortal. He's far too honorable to think such a thing. I suppose I could assist in arranging their executions."

"Michael!" Amata exclaimed through pursed lips. "This is not time for your games."

"Oh Amata, there is always time for games," Mandubratius drawled as he glanced over at Máire. "Honestly, I jest, I jest. I will see about arranging for their release."

"Thank you so—" his redheaded guest began to say.

"Ah, ah, ah," Mandubratius interjected with a smirk He rose from his chair and walked over to stand in front of Máire... such an odd name for a beautiful woman. "I have one condition that you must meet." He stared down at her green eyes, trying to stop imagining what pleasures her pouting lips could bring him. He stuck out his right hand instead. "Kiss my ring."

"This is... this must be a joke," Máire said. Her right brow lifted in a questioning arc. He vaguely remembered seeing the General in his days as a mortal make that very gesture. She must have copied her sponsor.

"Either my ring or my arse," Mandubratius replied, grinning down at her. "It is entirely up to you, Maél... Máire."

He watched her purse her lips. She then leaned forward, and he felt a soft brush of air on his ring finger. She avoided touching the gold, though of course he knew it was toxic to Deargh Du. As Máire sat back up, he noticed a pained expression on her face.

He then turned to face Amata.

She started to chuckle. "You do not expect me to kiss your ring, do you, Michael?"

He stuck his hand in front of her and stared into her blue eyes.

"I only do this because we do not have time," Amata groaned at him. She leaned forward and kissed it.

"Well, then it is settled. Now I must change into more courtly attire. The emperor and his courtiers do love dressing like their subjects, but they expect decoration from the visitors, and you two make me look very poor indeed." He went into the bedroom and began to dress.

Mandubratius emerged a few moments later. "Shall we go?"

"Oh how the mighty have fallen. Hello, Praetor."

A familiar voice swelled through the cell in Greek, making Marcus twitch a little as he sat up. The darkness cleared from his brain.

"Where have I heard that voice before," he muttered.

He could smell Máire and Amata. The third blood-drinker, a Lamia, remained a mystery for the moment. Marcus sat up in bed and stared back at Máire. Her face revealed strong displeasure. Then the stranger nudged her aside to look at him. The stranger's face grew familiar, and he realized he remembered the voice.

"Man–" he began.

"My name is Michael Tolomei," Mandubratius replied, now in Latin. "I am the papal emissary to the Imperial Court. I understand that you are Marcus of Bath. Perhaps we met during my visits to churches in Wessex. Oh and I must apologize, for I have brought your friends, Lady Amata and Lady Maél Muire to join me. Such lovely friends you have, Marcus."

Marcus watched the Briton smile at him.

Did he ever not have a game to play?

"Am I to understand that you and your cohorts are possessed by Satan?" the newly renamed Michael asked him.

"Mandubratius," he drawled, "stop with this ridiculous game." He walked up to the door and peeked through the bars, ignoring his earlier orders to himself about wasting his remaining energy. He then placed his hands on the bars.

Máire pushed Mandubratius aside and reached for Marcus' hand. Her fingertips brushed over his knuckles.

Mandubratius shoved Máire to the side. "I am not quite sure I believe you, sir," Mandubratius challenged with a smile. "Also, you mistake me for some associate of yours. My name is Michael, and the inspector general himself claims to have seen you preparing to drink the life essence from another man."

"The inspector general is blind," Marcus hissed. "He is mistaken. When will he finish this fool's game?" he addressed Amata and Máire.

Marcus watched 'Michael' wipe his face with a handkerchief. "My, you do not have to be so rude and spit in my face. You are quite the barbarian. If you will behave that way, then I will not help you out of here. Shall we, ladies?"

Marcus noticed stares exchanged between the women.

"My lord, I think these men do not appear to be the children of the devil. Perhaps this Inspector General is mistaken in what he witnessed," Amata countered.

Marcus rubbed his forehead, bewildered that Amata seemed to play along in this game.

"Mmmmm, perhaps," Amata's brother-in-darkness purred. "However, these men could be Satan's helpers. They can be hiding the truth. Perhaps executing them at first light will prevent further deaths in the empire."

He watched Máire turn to face Mandubratius. "You promised assistance. I kissed your ring, my lord. Do you mean just to jest again? After all, there are continuing attacks in the empire, are there not? Does that not prove these men are innocent?" She delivered her last words in a derisive hiss. "My impatience with this game has reached a summit!" she yelled in British.

"Oh very well," Mandubratius groaned as he stared at Máire as if disappointed. "We will discuss this matter with the inspector general. Perhaps he could be persuaded that he made a mistake. Will you ladies accompany me?" Marcus watched Mandubratius' green eyes turn cold, "or would you rather remain in this dark, dank dungeon?"

"I will go, Papal Emissary." A quick and false smile flitted across Máire's face. She turned to Marcus and leaned forward. "We will return with your freedom," she whispered.

They all backed away just when a guard approached them. "Get away from the bars!" the guard yelled at them. "You will be here for a long time," he shouted at Marcus with a sneer.

Marcus sat down against the wall adjacent to the other cell.

"It sounds like we may be leaving here soon," he said to Claudius.

"If Máire does not kill Mandubratius first," Claudius replied.

(Continued on page 103)

heather poinsett dunbar
and
christopher dunbar

Curse of Venus
Morrigan's Brood Book IV

Trade Paperback / 396 Pages / List Price $19.99 USD
Also available as an eBook for $4.99 USD

Excerpt includes scenes from pages 191 through 198

i am a child of the goddess morrigan...
i was born in the land of éire...
and my heart blazes with its fury...
i have lived through the ages...
i seek to right those who have wronged...
i am the maintainer of the balance...
the balance must be maintained

the strigoi, the cursed of venus, have spread through the holy roman empire and parts beyond like a plague. in response, pope leo iii takes advantage of the scourge to settle an old score with the man he placed on the throne: charlemagne. the pope leads the papal army into the heart of the empire and demands sovereignty over what he believes is a papal matter.

charlemagne disagrees, and soon papal and imperial forces stand face-to-face across the field of battle. will their leaders' bitter rivalry send the empire further into chaos and destruction, or will their deargh du "angels" save them from themselves, and from venus' cursed?

continue the journey... the fourth in a series of stories revolving around the deargh du through the ages.

Heather Poinsett Dunbar & Christopher Dunbar

chapter ten

Constantinople, 801 CE

(Excerpt begins on page 192)

"You still stink," Máire informed Mandubratius as soon as he opened the inn's door for them.

Mandubratius chuckled. "I know. I want to keep some memories of this evening fresh in my mind, and what better way than through my senses."

"It's not your senses that concern me," Máire quipped before wandering over to a bench with her family. After sitting down next to Julien, she noticed Edward and Amata with arms linked sauntering down the hallway towards the rooms. During their quick jaunt, they passed Marcus, who stormed into the common room looking for a fight.

As soon as her father-in-darkness saw Mandubratius, his eyes turned green and his face darkened. Fear welled up inside of her, for she rarely witnessed him unleash such anger.

Marcus grabbed Mandubratius, lifted him, and slammed him against the wall. A board behind the Lamia broke.

"How dare you initiate a coup while we're on a mission?" Marcus growled.

Máire stood up, as did most of the others.

A coup?

Mandubratius smiled and presented a boyish façade as he gazed at Marcus. "Well, it helped me succeed in obtaining the mirror."

"You set this up. You set up all of it! Just so you could regain control of this branch of the Lamia!" Marcus accused as he shook Mandubratius.

Máire noticed Patroclus remained seated.

What was his role in all of this?

Mandubratius coughed a little and then smiled. "I'm so flattered that you feel I could orchestrate these events over time and it would end with you holding me against the wall by my neck and tunic. However, I cannot claim that I had any hand in setting the Strigoi off on their murderous campaign." He laughed for a moment before calming. Soon, the Lamia's face projected seriousness. "But yes, everything else... I did," he drawled.

Máire had no idea that while Mandubratius fornicated and prattled on at the orgy that he was secretly orchestrating the fall of a government of blood-drinkers. She could not help but feel... impressed... in a sick, sad way.

Marcus stared at Mandubratius for a moment, before slowly lowering him to the floor. He then released Mandubratius and backed away. "Couldn't you have avoided staging this coup until after we had taken care of the Strigoi?" he asked.

"Marcus, my birthday is next week, and I wanted a united Lamia empire before then," Mandubratius replied while adopting a jovial visage.

Marcus did not appear to accept the response, for his eyes reverted to their otherworldly green and he reached out for the Lamia again.

"Before you demonstrate your strength again, Cu Chulainn, there is another, more logical reason for this coup."

Marcus lowered his arm and glared at Mandubratius. "I'm listening," he hissed, though his eyes remained green.

"Had I not initiated this coup, we wouldn't have the backing of the Children of Ares when we meet up with the Strigoi," Mandubratius replied.

"Are you saying that, now that you are back in control, they will fight alongside us?" Marcus asked.

"You may depend on it."

Marcus did not look convinced, but his expression softened and his eyes became bluish-gray again. He leaned against the table in a casual manner.

"So, how did you obtain the mirror?" he asked.

Mandubratius smiled. "The Basileus Irene and I traded for it."

"Traded what?" Marcus asked, though worry clouded his tone.

Máire interrupted them before Mandubratius could speak. "He transformed her," she said with vehemence, though she couldn't decide what aspect of this revelation harmed her the most.

"Sponsored, actually," Mandubratius corrected. "I made Empress Irene a Lamia. So, what of it? Oh, and she'll realize a few hours after sundown that becoming a Lamia does not increase one's beauty and youth. After looking at Amata, Fianait, and Máire, she seemed to assume that you were all Lamia."

Marcus sat down in apparent shock.

"What are you saying?" Claudius asked.

"I'm saying we must flee at sunset with haste," Mandubratius answered.

"Why?" Julien asked.

"Because, youngling, Irene's vanity is as volatile as Greek fire," Mandubratius answered.

"Won't the Children of Ares protect you?" Arwin asked before taking a sip of what Máire assumed was unadulterated wine, knowing his preferences.

Mandubratius shrugged. "Perhaps, but they owe fidelity to her as well, and there is a rather universal saying about a woman scorned."

Marcus stood back up... always a man of action. "Then, we need to leave now! The Children of Ares know where we are, and I'm sure your new child knows it, too. If we're caught during the day in this inn, the Empress will figure out a way to bring us into the sun, if she's as volatile as you say she is." His tone belied his irritation.

Mandubratius shrugged. "Yes, I'm sure that is a good idea. She has men castrated for not pleasing her. She has executed men for daring to say she was over twenty-five seasons. Look what she did to her own son for daring to have an opinion of his own. Despite what you might think, playing this game was necessary to snatch the mirror."

"That's enough from you," Marcus growled. "First a coup, and now you're lying to the sovereign of these lands about her new gifts!"

At that moment, a disheveled Amata rejoined them. The Lamia frowned at Mandubratius and added, "I truly hope there are no consequences from this ill-conceived sponsorship."

"Ill-conceived? Look, we needed the mirror, and I took the risk. She's mad, but she won't catch up to us, and if she does, well... our friends will carry the Lamia away, Amata. Besides, Irene finds me charming. She'll move past this minor annoyance," Mandubratius countered.

"Let's stop flapping our gums and leave. We'll have to sleep underground, outside of the city," Arwin grumbled before tipping his goblet back and chugging the rest of its contents.

"How about the sewers," Edward suggested, though Máire didn't find sleeping in sewers to be the best option. It required hours of thorough scrubbing to scour the stink away.

Instead, she added her own recommendation. "I remember seeing a cemetery outside of the walls."

"Both places are far too obvious," Claudius answered.

"True," Marcus admitted. "Any other suggestions?"

"How about the ocean," Fianait suggested, but then she seemed to recognize the holes in her proposal. "Oh," she muttered while looking over the Ekimmu Cruitne and shook her head. "Sorry, I forgot."

Marcus sighed. "I think our only option is to fly to the west, as quickly as we can. Then we'll land and dig in when we need to."

So much for feeling clean after my hot bath. You owe me, Mandubratius.

When Irene awoke the next morning, she shivered from the cool, pre-dawn chill. A quick glance around the room revealed that dawn soon approached. She sat up, slid out of her bed, and walked towards the nearest window, hoping the sun might warm her.

She stuck her right hand out the window and waited for the sun to kiss the top of her outstretched hand.

When the sun rose high enough, she watched in awe as its light touched buildings and trees far away. Soon, the wave of brightness rushed closer to the palace. Once the bright wave washed the palace with light, a beam of sunlight pierced through her window and bathed her outstretched hand.

However, instead of feeling a kiss, the sun burned her hand as if she had thrust it into a bed of glowing embers. Irene screamed from the intense pain and stared in stupefaction as her hand began to smoke and crisp.

Servants and guards rushed in. One of them poured water onto her hand.

"Get out! Leave me!" she roared at them, as she backed away from the window into the shadows of the Porphyra. Still, the bright sunlight hurt her eyes, so she looked away from the bright parts of the room.

Once she found a spot of relative darkness, Irene studied her hand again. Thankfully, her clouded mind began to clear. Soon, memories of the celebration last night came back to her. Mandubratius had arrived with three beauties, and he sought her mirror. Then she remembered being intimate with him… one of few men who could sate her needs. The sex was even better after…

He must have sponsored me!

Irene smiled and raced to find a mirror, wishing to see her renewed beauty.

Youth forever!

Giving up the sun seemed a small price to pay. While in the midst of searching through her dressing table, which stood bereft of her prized mirror, she felt her stomach growl, and she forgot about the mirror.

Irene tried to remember what Mandubratius had told her about consuming blood. The thought of drinking blood seemed sickening, at first, but her growing hunger quashed all misgivings. She needed blood… now.

"I need bandages and clean water!" Irene called out, as a means to summon a food source. While much of her experience last night remained blurry, she began to remember some instructions about feeding.

A servant arrived with a basin of water and set it down on the floor near where Irene cowered. She began binding Irene's arm.

Irene stopped the servant and murmured, "Stay for a moment." Her hunger had increased, and she could no longer ignore it. Along with her heightened hunger, she heard a loud pounding echoing in her ears. Irene glanced at the servant and realized that the sound was the drumming of the woman's quickening heart.

Irene experienced no qualms about tasting the blood of others. She could recall a time during another orgy, when someone accidently cut a servant during his throes of passion. Irene had licked the blood from the cut in a moment of curiosity. Before, she had found the taste odd but intriguing, yet now, she found the sweet, appetizing smell to be intoxicating.

Irene knew she could no longer wait… she had to taste blood, not only to fend off her hunger, but also because she imagined it tasted like ambrosia.

When she locked eyes on her servant, the girl lowered her gaze.

"Look me in the eyes," Irene commanded in a soft tone.

The servant made eye contact with her again, and Irene witnessed fear.

"Calm down," she said. Almost immediately, Irene could hear the servant's heart slow.

"How may I serve you?" the young woman asked in a low stutter.

"I am hungry," Irene murmured.

"Let me get you some… food," the servant muttered, attempting to step away, but Irene had gently seized the woman's left arm with her right hand.

The Empress smiled. "But you've already brought me food, my dear."

"I did?"

Irene pulled the serving girl close enough to her that mere inches of space existed between the two women. "Yes, silly girl. I mean to feed from you!"

Before the servant girl could scream, Irene grabbed her mouth with her left hand and pulled the girl's body against hers. Then she felt her teeth extend, as if it were some kind of reflex. With her prey effectively immobilized by her newfound strength, Irene bit the servant girl's throat and feasted upon the blood that poured out. With each pulse of blood that passed her lips, Irene could feel energy grow within her. The rush of warmth… of power… drowned out all other thoughts.

As Irene drained the servant, she could feel the girl's heart begin to slow, and soon it stopped completely, along with the flow of blood.

Irene stared at the empty expression in the servant's dead eyes for a moment and then tossed her carcass across the room.

With her hunger now sated, Irene sauntered to the dressing desk once again to search for a mirror. Once she sat down, she noticed that the burn on her hand began to fade. "This is a miraculous gift," she whispered.

After searching through three drawers, Irene finally found a small mirror. She giggled at the discovery and held up the mirror so she could stare at herself and witness the fruits of Mandubratius' gift… eternal youth and beauty.

Instead of a striking maiden, an old hag stared at her in the mirror. She screamed at the unchanged reflection of her face.

I remain old!

"You Liar!" she yelled at the top of her lungs.

Guards and servants rushed into her room to protect her, but when they saw the dead servant, they started yelling.

Irene covered her mouth, unsure of how to hide her elongated teeth, and remembered that she needed to take care of potential exposure before they suspected anything.

"That girl tried to kill me! I punished her. Take her body away and bury it in a pauper's grave!"

Two of the guards grabbed the dead servant's body and hauled it out of the room. Servants rushed in to clean up blood and re-polish the floor.

While the servants busied themselves with their work, Irene thought back to her conversation with Mandubratius, shortly after her sponsorship.

Mandubratius did warn me to try not to kill them.

He had whispered that it would taste exquisite to drain them, but it would give her a headache afterwards because of the problems stemming from death.

"I suppose I should take that advice," she grumbled in what she hoped to be an inaudible tone.

"What is your desire, Imperial Majesty?" the guard captain asked.

Irene rolled her tongue around in her mouth to make sure her teeth had retracted. "Leave me," she told him. After a moment of introspection, an idea occurred to her. "No, wait!" Irene threw up her hands and paced through the darkest shadows of the room. "Cover up my windows, then find Aetios!"

As the guards and servants went about their new duties, Irene paced and planned while waiting for Aetios to appear. Soon, thick blankets tacked over wooden frames sealed with plaster held out most of the sun's deadly rays.

What should I do to make Mandubratius pay for abandoning me once again, when I needed his assistance to survive?

Rapid footsteps heralded Aetios' arrival. After closing the door behind him, he kneeled and said, "I am at your service, my Empress."

Irene at first didn't look at him. While staring at a distant tapestry, she said, "Aetios. You've served me well as my secretary during my many orgies."

"I am happy you appreciate my service, and I hope to continue to serve you in this capacity," he groveled.

Tedious man, but useful… unlike his predecessor, who feeds the worms.

"You may yet… Do you recollect the man I allowed in my chambers last night?" she asked.

Aetios nodded his head. "Yes, Imperial Majesty."

"Do you remember his carriage?"

"Yes, Basileus. It's from an inn near the outside of town. I think it's called the Byzantine Inn."

Irene smiled. "Well done. Your memory is excellent. Send an army detachment to detain all the patrons, staff, and the owner. Bring them in for questioning. If they offer resistance, subdue them, and if necessary, kill them."

Aetios bowed. "Yes, Imperial Majesty." He then departed the Porphyra.

With her room now empty of servants and guards, living or dead, Irene gripped the small mirror in both hands and stared into its depths. "Soon, Mandubratius, I will hold your severed genitals in my hand and bask in the beauty of my mirror," Irene swore.

Time drifted by with scant change in her appearance. Irene neither aged nor grew younger. She had hoped that perhaps Mandubratius had spoken the truth, that she would be beautiful and young again… that the transformation just needed time to run its course. However, after an unknown number of hours staring at her reflection, Irene felt her hope die.

I am the blithering fool for having such hope.

With as much fury as she could muster, Irene gripped the top of the mirror in her right hand and squeezed with all of her might. The mirror broke with a satisfying crunch. After shattering it, she held the mangled mirror in her right hand and rested her face in her left.

Irene ignored the temptation to stare into the broken shards of the mirror again. She doubted there would be any change. She would always look old. Gray hairs and age spots would remain. This existence seemed torturous.

Even though the pains of age have faded, what difference does it make?

The sound of footsteps running towards her bedroom brought her attention to the door.

In walked a messenger, who bowed and then lowered himself in complete prostration.

"Yes? What is it?" she asked, weary of visitors in her current state.

"Please pardon the presence of your most humble servant, Basileus, but the captain of the guards found the residents of the inn. He has brought them here for you to interrogate."

Irene pulled herself away from her pity and said, "Bring them in here. I shall confront them myself."

The messenger rose slowly, and then he then turned and scrambled away.

Irene fixed her eyes on the largest mirror shard she held and glared at her reflection again. In her gaze, she focused her burning rage on Mandubratius, willing this bit of mirror to melt. Because the shard didn't obey her will, she flung it as far and as hard as she could towards the far wall.

When the shard slammed into the wall, it embedded itself in the marble.

The staccato of many booted feet and the smell of sweat preceded the arrival of guards, who barged through the door. When they saw that she was not in danger, they looked around, confused.

Irene stood up and yelled, "What is the meaning of this?"

One of the guards, the captain's second-in-command, said, "Basileus, we heard a loud noise and thought that you were being attacked."

"Do I look as if I've been attacked?" Irene growled.

(Continued on page 198)

Heather Poinsett Dunbar
and
Christopher Dunbar
Shards of Light
Morrigan's Brood Book V

Trade Paperback / # Pages TBD / List Price $TBD USD
Also available as an eBook for $TBD USD

Excerpt contains scenes from pages ~68 through ~73

I am a child of the goddess Morrigan...
I was born in the land of Éire...
and my heart blazes with its fury...
I have lived through the ages...
I seek to right those who have wronged...
I am the maintainer of the balance...
the balance must be maintained

Many sets of eyes peer through the mist, watching events unfold as the dark alliance seeks out an ancient device that they hope will uncorrupt the menace that has nearly brought the Holy Roman Empire to its knees. However, not everyone beyond the mist is content merely to watch.

The scourge continues unchecked, but instead of murdering innocent people, Venus' cursed are capturing them and transforming them into more devils and demons. The strigoi are no longer bands of shambling hordes... they are now an army.

Can the dark alliance cobble together a sufficient force of arms to combat the scourge, or will betrayal and bitter rivalries seek to topple the empire into the void?

Continue the journey... the fifth in a series of stories revolving around the Deargh Du through the ages.

---

chapter four

(Excerpt begins on page 68)

The lightning had not behaved. Then again, lightning never acted with a predictable nature. Even though the smell of burned hair lingered and served as a distraction to her commands, the wind now asked for release.

Máire inhaled and exhaled as she felt the passion of the old knowledge consume her. The thrill of channeling energy from the opened path to the Otherworld made her experience a strange giddiness she had not felt in ages. She rolled up the scrolls and placed them within the leather case.

Máire scanned the valley, looking for a safe place to unleash the wind. She soon found a gentle slope where the vortex of wind could settle. With her spot selected, Máire concentrated on summoning thunder and gathering breezes.

Animals in the valley below screeched, annoyed with another one of her interruptions, and began to race for the forest.

Máire studied the point of the valley that she wished the tip of the vortex to touch and then dissipate. A simple chant came to her thoughts, and before she could think over the words, they pushed past her lips in a fevered hurry.

Máire closed her eyes, envisioning clouds coming together, blotting out the stars and moon. She sensed the center of the windstorm gather speed and lower towards the ground. She opened her eyes and stared at the center of the vortex. Trees whipped and began bending to the ground as if in obeisance to the force of nature.

The sound of shattering limbs and trunks made Máire cringe in fear. She could no longer concentrate on controlling the vortex. The debris within its many arms of wind churned and whipped about, raining stones in her direction.

"Go back through the passage," she murmured, hoping that her words would be enough to send the energy back through the gateway to the Otherworld.

Suddenly, searing pain tore through her body. Máire felt the winds lift her and toss her about like a dry leaf. A heavy thud resonated around her, and she realized the winds had forced her into the dirt and rocks. A tremendous roar echoed in her ears. "Please," she whispered. "Return to your home."

Whether through command or coincidence, the storm began to dissipate and lose its integrity.

Did it hear my request?

Máire rolled onto her back and closed her eyes.

Máire awoke to hear the sounds of licking and slurping. She felt a rough tongue lick over her curls.

Is Lucius grooming me now?

Soon a warm weight rested on her chest, and then the coarse tongue began to lap over a sore spot on her forehead.

She finally opened her eyes and found the land bathed in sunlight. She attempted to bring her right hand to shade her eyes, but her palm could not move past soft fur.

Máire blinked a few times, allowing her eyes to grow accustomed to the light. A glance to where she felt the furry mass pressing against her revealed a black cat, which leaned in closer, nosing her hand away, and returned to tending her wound. She heard and felt its delicate purr grow louder.

Lucius has a throaty purr, so perhaps another cat has found me.

As she patted the cat, it looked up and studied her with bicolor gold and green eyes.

Definitely not Lucius.

When it flopped onto its side, Máire followed her compulsion to rub the cat's belly. She then looked up, while continuing to stroke the cat, and studied the large, white clouds above. With each touch, the cat purred louder. Soon she discerned the sounds of other animals echoing through the air.

As she pushed herself up off the ground, the cat squeaked a meow as if disturbed that Máire had deigned to move her. Once on her feet, she surveyed her surroundings and discovered an impressive dun set in the distance. Sun gleamed from its white stone walls. It stood as the tallest building of her memory. "A truly mighty fortress," she whispered, when a shadow fell, offering immediate shade. Máire looked up to find the source of the shade... into a graceful face... and then lurched to her knees.

Upon knowing who blocked the sun, she stared into Her black eyes and asked, "Phant... Morr...grandmother? Have I passed into the Otherworld?" Máire soon felt a warm hand stroke her hair.

"Arise, my granddaughter," Morrigan sang in a gentle voice that soothed Máire's fears. "Fear not. Yet next time, be mindful of Brigid's place in your lap. I do not think she liked being dumped to the ground, when you moved to your knees."

Máire turned and studied the black cat, which narrowed her eyes at her. While Máire watched, the graceful feline figure changed, transforming into a blonde woman who stared at her with a strange smile.

"You are most fortunate that you give good rubs," purred the blonde woman, who pouted as She spoke. "I felt like clawing you when you cast me aside. Well, stand up and close your mouth, Deargh Du. Honestly, you and your father-in-darkness tend to gawk at me in the most amusing fashion."

Máire found her feet and rose. "I am sorry. I am confused. I was flung to the ground, and I lost consciousness. I awoke here, and I'm not sure of myself."

"Have no worries, granddaughter, for you have not passed. I simply-"

The clearing of Brigid's throat interrupted Morrigan.

She chuckled. "Fine, Brigid. We decided to bring you here, Máire, to discuss your new knowledge."

At that moment, the wind began to roar, assaulting Máire's ears, forcing her to cover them. Thunder rumbled and lightning blinded her. Máire nearly fell back to her knees as a God appeared from a beam of bright, gleaming light, which had come down from the maelstrom above.

"Ladies, stop proclaiming your actions in this matter. I am He who called this one forth. I wished to see she who dared to ask for my energy." The God tipped His head to the side to study Máire.

"True, but we planned on speaking with her," Brigid countered.

Morrigan reached the God of the Sea in two long strides, placed Her right hand on Máire's left shoulder, and said, "Now Manannán, this is no mere mortal. She's my granddaughter... and one of my Deargh Du."

"She's an excellent druid," Brigid added.

Máire studied the ground, feeling her face redden at the compliments. When she looked up, she could see Manannán Mac Lir smiling at her with a crooked grin.

"I was surprised," said the God. "It has been... at least as the mortals perceive it... a very long time since one has called for my energy. I feared that the knowledge of such matters had died with the growing popularity of Je and Hovah's son. Sometimes I fear that my name has melted into obscurity."

Morrigan patted His shoulder and stated, "Well, we have made sure that our names will not be lost. We gathered all the mortals' knowledge from before, and we entrusted it to a group of mortal druids. They have been passing on that knowledge from generation to generation. They secreted away copies, in case that knowledge was discovered by those who might destroy it."

Brigid slinked Her way towards Manannán in a manner most befitting a cat. "By a strange twist of fate..."

Morrigan cleared Her throat.

"Oh fine," Brigid grumbled. "Morrigan felt it was time to release a set of scrolls in Vézelay. The scroll moved into this Deargh Du's hands."

"Part of that knowledge involves invocation of your name to call forth the tornado," Morrigan said.

"Tornado?" Máire whispered. The three deities stared at her in a strange manner. "I am not familiar with that word, please excuse my interruption." She felt like a small child surrounded by knowledgeable and somewhat frightening adults.

Morrigan laughed. "For Dana's sake, Máire, you may speak. In a different time, the vortex you created is called 'tornado'."

"I wish I could have witnessed it first hand," Manannán sighed. "I imagine it would have been so beautiful."

A small feeling of dread grew in the pit of Máire's stomach. The vortex or tornado had been so hard to control and destructive.

"Máire, call forth another one," Morrigan said.

Máire could see Manannán's sea-colored eyes gleam at the thought of that.

"Yes, please do so, Máire. I want to see it," He said.

"I don't feel as if I could control it."

"Are you disobeying your grandmother?" A playful grin lit Morrigan's face.

"No, no," Máire said, feeling a large amount of nervous energy grow within. "However, the experience of calling down such a great force has humbled me."

"And so it should have," Brigid said.

"In order to master this knowledge, you must practice it," Morrigan stated. "Then you can learn to control it. Who best to help you in this than the Lord of Winds, Sea, and Travel?"

Manannán scoffed. "My duties are more than merely that!"

The Goddesses smiled at Him.

"My apologies," Morrigan purred. "I was merely teasing you."

Máire studied Their faces, wondering what games occurred between the Tuaths. They turned back to her with somewhat patronizing grins, as if she were a young child learning to take steps.

"Alright," Máire said. "I will summon the vortex." She closed her eyes.

"Ah, ah." A hand gripped hers, and she felt a soothing heat. Máire opened her eyes, feeling Manannán's stare.

"You must not think of the size of the storm, young Deargh Du," the God whispered. His fingers unfolded her hand and He raised her palm towards the warming rays of the gentle golden orb above. "Rather, you should think of this vortex fitting into your palm. Then, you will control it by closing and opening your hand. The vortex will abide by your thoughts," Manannán continued. "If you think of it as a larger being than what you can contain in your hand, it will revert to its own nature. The vortex's destructive force will unlock, and you will not be able to direct it."

Máire nodded her head. "I will try."

"Trying will not work with nature. While you cannot fully control the energy you summon, you may guide it," Brigid said.

"Then, I will do so," Máire said, sounding more confident than she felt. Steeling herself, she closed her eyes. The simple chant came to her lips again, summoning the vortex to the glade in the distance.

She closed her hand, envisioning the clouds joining and blotting the sun.

Then slowly, Máire spread her hand open. The spiraling windstorm gathered speed and lowered towards the ground. She opened her eyes and stared at the center of the vortex. A strange realization came to her mind as it grew in strength. It seemed more willing to listen this time. A voice within begged her to release the full power of the storm, but she ignored the urge.

A strange sound echoed near her. She noticed the God and Goddesses hitting Their hands together and looking pleased.

Máire turned away from the minor distraction, her focus centered on her right palm. She closed her hand and whispered for the energy to return to its origin.

A warming force surrounded her as she felt arms envelope her. Morrigan patted her back.

"Just remember to put these skills to good purpose, granddaughter. Do not abuse them, for they are not toys."

Morrigan kissed her forehead and pulled away. Manannán's eyes engulfed her, and she found herself unable to speak. She could vaguely remember her nights of mortality and feeling overwhelmed by the Deargh Du. This seemed a thousand times over that engulfing beauty.

"Thank you for calling my name. Do so again when it is necessary. Seldom do I hear it. I relish it."

"I will do so," she murmured, feeling foolish for not finding words.

"Ladies, I feel someone calling for my boat," Manannán said.

Máire watched His smile linger on the Goddesses for a moment before His body melded with the winds. He faded into a small vortex.

Brigid yawned, "After that fine display, I could use a nap." She stretched Her form and reverted into the black cat. The Goddess leapt up towards Máire. Máire inhaled as Brigid landed in her arms.

A rather insistent purr echoed.

"Now, I want the attention you normally give Lucius," the cat demanded.

Máire stared at Morrigan in disbelief that she cradled a Goddess in her arms. Stroking the black fur, she found herself yawning.

"You are sleepy and need to rest," Morrigan said. "Remember to maintain the balance. Do not abuse the knowledge, or else the balance may seek you."

Máire sat down on the green grasses.

"I promise, grandmother," she whispered. "I love you." She leaned back and enjoyed the cushion of the Otherworld as it cradled her.

"I'm so glad you realize that you have that power as well." Morrigan crouched down. "I love you, too. Now, please tell Marcus that he has the power to overcome his nightmares. They are visions, not reality."

Brigid's resounding purr soothed Máire as she closed her eyes.

(Continued on page 73)

published and future works

Title	Synopsis	Release
Morrigan's Brood Morrigan's Brood Book I	Éire is invaded by a race of blood-drinkers seeking an artifact they believe will restore them to power. Yet the Dearg Du, the protectors of Éire, are not prepared to defend the island. Only with the help of a Roman general from an earlier time can they hope to rise up against the invaders.	Dec. 2009 Re-print Jan. 2012
Crone of War Morrigan's Brood Book II	The Lamia expeditionary force has gained a foothold in Éire and has formed an alliance with a powerful Irish chieftain and his malevolent mother. To reinforce them, a massive Lamia army, which is departing Rome, will soon give them enough power to conquer Éire and find their lost treasure. Will the Dearg Du and their new-found friends be able to protect Éire from the invaders, or will the Dearg Du's suspicion of other blood-drinkers allow their enemies to be victorious?	July 2010 Re-print Aug. 2012
Madness & Reckoning Madness - Short-Story	Following the events of 564 CE, madness strikes one of the Lamia's most important personages. Can the Lamia march on, or will this insanity cast them into civil war?	eBook Apr. 2011 Print Feb. 2012
Madness & Reckoning Reckoning - Short-Story	Following the events of 564 CE, the Dearg Du must come to grips with change or see old strife resurface, which could tear the Dearg Du apart.	eBook June 2011 Print Feb. 2012
Dark Alliance Morrigan's Brood Book III	A new menace threatens the Balance within the Holy Roman Empire as vicious murders of both mortals and blood-drinkers spread throughout the empire like wildfire. Can a hastily formed alliance between archenemies thwart this new menace, or will festering hatred bring about the empire's doom?	Sept. 2011
Curse of Venus Morrigan's Brood Book IV	The Strigoi, the Cursed of Venus, have spread through the Holly Roman Empire and parts beyond like a plague. In response, Pope Leo III takes advantage of the scourge to settle an old score with the man he placed on the throne: Charlemagne. Will their bitter rivalry send the Empire further into chaos and destruction, or will their Dearg Du "angels" save them from themselves and from Venus' Cursed?	June 2013
Shards of Light Morrigan's Brood Book V	Many sets of eyes peer through the mist, watching events unfold as the dark alliance seeks out an ancient device that they hope will uncorrupt the menace that has nearly brought the Holy Roman Empire to its knees. However, not everyone beyond the mist is content merely to watch.	June 2016

Future Morrigan's Brood Series titles include Dynasties of Night (Book 6), Odin's Chosen (Book 7), and Hera's Wrath (Book 8), all of which are in progress.

Other works include It's in the Cards (a novella that will appear within an anthology with other authors, in queue for publication) and A Year and a Day (novel, on hold).

about the authors

Heather Poinsett Dunbar

Born in Houston, Texas, Heather began writing her first book at age eight. While her grammatical structure left much to be desired, she continued to hone her writing and storytelling skills. During a college internship in London, England, her curiosity about ancient cultures and mythology intensified. She backpacked through Europe, fell in love with Scotland, cried at the retelling of part of Ulster cycle, garnered ghost stories from the Beefeaters at the Tower, wandered the Roman ruins in Bath, and danced around the stones in Avebury.

After spending all her spare time studying these new interests in many libraries and on the road, she began working on her masters in Library and Information Science at the University of North Texas. She now resides in the Houston area with her husband and three cats. She loves exploring the local culture as well as the many Celtic festivals and events in Texas. She now works as a librarian for a small, local college, and her favorite authors include Morgan Llewellyn, Neil Gaiman, Terry Pratchett, Evelyn Vaughn, Alison Weir, and Randy Lee Eickhoff.

Christopher Dunbar

Chris Dunbar was born in Greenport, Long Island, New York and then moved to Texas as soon as he could, at least that is the story he tells to native Texans, such as his wife. Chris keeps searching for ways to leave Houston, like moving to Auburn, Alabama, Dallas, and even San Antonio, but Houston just keeps reeling him back. Chris' day job is performing Business Continuity and Disaster Recovery, but his night job is coming up with creative ways to wound and maim the characters he and his wife Heather created. For fun, Chris enjoys the occasional novel and video game, but he also likes to delve into his Scottish ancestry and tool leather. When he can find the time, Chris pretends to play the Bodhran and the didgeridoo, much to the chagrin of his cats Lucius, Ophelia, and Clyde, not to mention his wife Heather. Chris is also an avid wearer of the kilt.

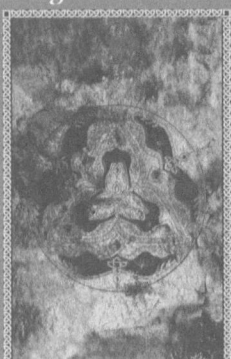

MORRIGAN'S BROOD
MORRIGAN'S BROOD Book I

heather poinsett dunbar
& christopher dunbar

CRONE OF WAR
MORRIGAN'S BROOD Book II

heather poinsett dunbar
& christopher dunbar

MADNESS & RECKONING
Stories of the morrigan's brood series

heather poinsett dunbar
& christopher dunbar

Welcome to the Books of the Morrigan's Brood Series, Written by Heather Poinsett Dunbar and Christopher Dunbar

Dark Alliance
Morrigan's Brood Book III

heather poinsett dunbar
& christopher dunbar

Curse of Venus
Morrigan's Brood Book IV

heather poinsett dunbar
& christopher dunbar

Shards of Light
Morrigan's Brood Book V

Coming
in
2016

heather poinsett dunbar
& christopher dunbar